The Tall Man

A small orb of bright light danced across the darkened room. Outside the blackness of night-time covered the gardens and hedgerows like a blanket.

Inside the bedroom the bed creaked.

The air had turned icy.

Her long, auburn hair lay tussled upon her pillow and Melody knew what she would see when she opened her sleep filled eyes.

He was sat, hunched, at the end of the bed. He wasn't looking at her, his eyes were gazing off into the distance somewhere, to some far-off land, another place in the vast universe of space, another time even.

She could see that his skin was covered in a million wrinkles, but he had a kind face. He looked to be wearing a big, thick, cable knit jumper with big buttons over a plaid shirt. His brown trousers looked worn but comfortable and there were just a few strands of grey hair on his mostly bald head. He was old, very old. Who knew how old? He could have been any age. Melody could never tell how old they were.

That was not her gift.

The bed did not dip where the old man sat. The duvet was ruffled but that was from Melody's feet. The cheap, wood-effect dressing table was behind the old man and cluttered with her belongings, but Melody could see everything that sat upon it; her hairbrush, her make-up, her worn out diary from all those late-night entries, her perfume bottles, and her hair straighteners. Everything! Right through him! And he shimmered.

Gift! Some gift Melody thought to herself as she sat looking through the old man. Although all the hairs on her body were standing up and her neck tingled, Melody was not afraid.

The old man had been sitting on the end of her bed every night this week. That usually meant only one thing. He needed help. They always needed help. They, being the ones that had crossed over, the echoes of the past, the spirits, call them what you will.

People, Melody's friends mostly, friends of friends sometimes and occasionally any old Tom, Dick or Harry wanted to know about Melody's gift, if she were down the pub on a Saturday night. Usually someone got wind of it.

"Well how does it work?"

"Why is it you can see them, but we can't?"

And the favourite, most asked question, "Can you see my Aunty Doris?"

Melody was never sure why it was always Aunty Doris. Maybe there was some inside joke that she hadn't been told or maybe, just maybe, everyone did have an Aunty Doris. Except her!

"Come on love!" said her mum. "You need to go back to sleep. There's no one standing next to the cupboard. Will it help if I leave the light on?"

"No Mummy. He's still there with or without the light on but don't turn it off." Said the six-year-old Melody.

She had not felt an ounce of fear that first time. She should have and she had realised as she grew up that that was probably the one thing that made her mother doubt her the most initially. She had heard her father after her mother had explained it to him.

"What do you mean, there's somebody stood in her bedroom, but there's no one there. You're not making any sense woman. Why isn't she scared? Is she ok? Has she lost her marbles?"

"I think," her mother paused for effect. She loved to add the drama. "I think it's one of those make-believe friends. I've heard that lots of children her age has them. She'll grow out of it.

That had been twenty-one years ago, and Melody was still waiting to 'grow out of it'.

The old man was still sat there, glowing faintly at the foot of her bed.

An owl hooted somewhere off into the distance and the breeze carried the screech of a fox across the park land near her home. As the heat of the evening left her apartment, the walls pinged and popped, their nightly ritual of settling back down to where they belonged as they cooled.

Melody had tried to speak to the old man, but she knew when she had that it would be a waste of time. She could never speak to any of them until they were ready to speak to her. When he was ready it would all come blurting out one way or another.

Some spirits would show her a movie reel, inside her mind, others would show her simple pictures of random objects and others, the screamers as she liked to call them, would scream and shout at her until their story had been heard.

Until it happened Melody could only hazard a guess as to what sort of spirit it would be and as nothing was happening at that moment, Melody snuggled back under the duvet, closed her eyes, and started counting back from one hundred. She didn't get past seventy-four before sleep had taken her back within its grasp.

Her days were usually quieter and this one had been no different. Sometimes she would see people on the bus. It was only when other passengers sat on them or walked through them that she knew it was one of them.

If she ever caught the train, and she had to fairly regularly, she would often see them stood on the side of the track. Reliving the moment just before life pushed them to do the unthinkable. These apparitions made her feel the saddest. It was as though all the turmoil that was flooding their brains in those last passing moments were hurled through the train window at her. If only her friends down the pub could feel those emotions too, they certainly would not say she had a gift then. Thankfully the feelings only lasted with her for seconds, any longer with them in her head and she thought she might one day end up with them on the side of the track.

But today had gone by without a visitation, without even a glimpse into that other realm. Melody enjoyed these rare days, but it never lasted long, and that night was no exception.

As Melody lay snuggled up in her bed that night, the pillow smelling of detergent and fresh air, the stench hit her with such force that she threw back the covers and dashed to the toilet, only just making it before all her tea hurtled back down the pan.

She splashed cold water upon her face and sat on the edge of the bath, trying to muster up the courage to head back to her room. She had never had a visitation like that before. Every nerve ending tingled, and her head was slightly spinning, like an over-wound clock.

After a couple of moments, she edged her way from the side of the bath to the bathroom door and peered out into the hallway. She could see her bedroom door stood wide open, her chair with the day's clothes chucked over it and her heels laying on the floor, but saw no silhouette in the doorway.

Since she had lived alone there was no one to rescue her, no one to call out to, to give her reassurance that it would be ok. She missed that, missed her parents enormously. What perplexed Melody the most was that in all the years since her parents' death, neither of them had come and sat on the foot of her bed in the middle of the night or sat silently as the number 47 trundled into town.

"Mum, Dad, if you can hear me, wherever you are, I could really do with a hand right now."

But no helping hand came, and Melody still had to get back into her bedroom and the cosy warm bed that beckoned her, that she desperately needed to be in.

She shivered.

The stench of rotting flesh began to creep along the landing. The sickly, sweet smell of death, not far away from where Melody stood, rooted to the spot. But still there was no figure, no shadow, no echo of a life lost.

Melody's mouth filled with water once more and her stomach started to contract as the sound of gagging rushed up and out of her throat. She didn't make it back to the toilet. Her legs just would not move so she threw up where she stood, right in the middle of the hallway. Thank goodness she had chosen wooden flooring rather than a nice thick piled carpet.

As she stood looking at the splattering all over the floor, with the stench of vomit now joining the stench of rotting flesh, Melody noticed something.

"Oh, Good Lord!"

Her eyes had grown to the size of dinner plates.

Melody had her views on religion but that was all they were, just views. Now however, she started praying silently in the darkness.

The light from the streetlight outside her flat, shone through the bathroom window just enough to throw a faint beam of light right across the slushy mess on the floor, and there, in the centre of that slushy mess was a footprint.

Melody recoiled at what she was seeing, edging back further into the bathroom. She knew it was futile closing the bathroom door. These things had no boundaries, did not worry about personal space or privacy. They just went where they wanted when they wanted.

For the first time since six-year-old Melody had seen the man standing next to her wardrobe, Melody sobbed. Fear had taken hold of her, and she had no idea how to pull this one around.

“What would you have done Mum?” Melody whispered into the cold, night air.

The light coursed through Melody’s bedroom window, and she stirred as the sound of the birds infested her brain. She rubbed her eyes and suddenly the events of the previous night flooded her mind. Had she been dreaming all along? The sour throat and the rancid taste in her mouth told her that she had lived through that terrifying ordeal even though Melody had no knowledge of how she had made it back to the bedroom and into that cosy warm bed.

Outside, Melody heard a car horn, honking impatiently and realisation dawned on her. She grabbed her phone.

“Be down in five” she typed into the box.

“I knew you’d be L8” came the reply.

“you’re always L8” pinged the next message.

Melody returned a sad face then jumped out of bed. As she got out onto the landing, the vomit still lay splattered across the floor with the footprint in the centre. What seemed bad during the night looked positively horrifying in the cold light of day. The footprint must have belonged to a giant and several footprints could be seen trailing down the corridor, sludging sick with every step it went.

"Change of plan! Come up! Now!"

Melody heard the noise of the car engine die and the buzzer screamed at her from the other end of the hallway, making her jump. Melody grabbed the remote from small, hallway table and pressed the button. The front door clicked open, and a firm hand pushed it the rest of the way.

The six-foot, walking shed stopped. His tanned features paled in the bright light as he looked down at the mess.

"Who the… what… is this a joke?"

Melody immediately realised what was going through Ethan's mind and she held up her hand.

"Before you get all macho on me and start jumping to the wrong conclusions, let me tell you what happened."

Ethan was a rugby playing, policeman. He had been called bobby, copper, pavement stomper and more recently po-po. That made her think of a children's programme from her childhood, not a brave upstanding, law enforcing officer. He had heard every story ever invented and he knew that Melody had this 'gift' but like all of her other friends and past lovers, Ethan had never seen any of the strange events that Melody had talked about.

But this!

This was different on so many levels!

Here, for the first time, was actual evidence. He had never doubted Melody, unlike her parents in the beginning but he liked tangible evidence and here it was. Well kind of!

He took some photos of the footprint with his phone. He wasn't sure why he was doing this. He knew this wasn't a case that could be solved. How do you catch somebody you cannot see and what would you book them for anyway?

As he did his thing, Melody got herself dressed. When PC Po-Po had finished taking his snaps, Melody set about cleaning up. The stench of the vomit hit her again and memories of the night before flooded her mind. However, as hard as she tried, she still had no recollection of what had happened after she had seen the footsteps heading along the hallway, or how she had got back to her bedroom.

She was retching again as she mopped up the mess.

"Out of the way. We will never get out of here at this rate!"

"Where are we going that's so urgent?" Melody enquired and even though she felt really queasy, a small smile played across her lips.

Ethan loved to surprise her. When he had a few days off, they all belonged to her. He had taken her to museums, art galleries, botanical gardens and occasionally, if the forecast was good, he would head to the nearest seaside town, and they would spend the day on the beach. These were her favourite days. Melody loved the beach. Melody loved the feel of the sand beneath her feet, between her toes and enjoyed the feel of the sun as it soaked into her skin.

He would often give her little clues as to where they might be heading but today, he just put his fingers to one side of his lips and zipped them shut.

Melody gazed out of the window as the world flashed by. Tall trees lined the road like sentinels on guard. Their high treetops and leafy branches tickling the bellies of the few fluffy clouds above. Most of the sky was as clear and blue as if they were in the Mediterranean. Seagulls swooped down over the fields, scavengers of the skies, on the hunt for food and they screeched as they bombed and soared.

It felt good to be out of the flat, Melody thought to herself, not wanting to return any time soon. As her mind drifted Melody found herself drifting in and out of sleep, the night before having left her more exhausted than she had realised. She heard Ethan humming away to his favourite song on the radio then she heard him gasp and cough. It hit her then too, that rancid, putrid stench.

Ethan pulled the car onto the side of the road while cars and lorries sped past. It wasn't the safest place to stop and definitely not a good place to have to get out. Litter from a waste bin spilled out of the top and heaped around the base. Little bits of paper had fluttered away on the breeze and had snagged in the nearby bushes. He leaned over Melody and pushed her door open.

“Get out Mel, I need some air and I need to climb out your side.”

From outside of the car, they both stood coughing. Melody could not believe that Ethan had experienced the stench too.

“I don’t understand how you can smell it too. You don’t see any of them, how is it you are smelling this. I thought the smell had just been put into my head, like the images and the voices.”

“Beats me but now I can see why you were so ill!”

He was still coughing and trying not to be sick himself. He had been to some cases of bodies that had been undiscovered for a few days and the stench was overpowering but this was something else.

“I need a pint, no make that two pints and a large whiskey!”

“You don’t drink!” Melody reminded him.

“You mean I used to not drink! That smell is enough to turn even the great saints to drink.”

Melody, after taking big gulps of clean, sweet smelling, fresh air, stuck her head back inside the Saab. The smell had gone, completely and there was no trace of anything or anyone inside. Melody decided that it was time to give her old friend Stella a call. As the Saab sped along, continuing their journey, Melody dialled her friend.

~

Stella was nearly in her sixties now but was the best psychic medium that she had ever met.

Melody's mum had first introduced Stella to her daughter when she'd had her initial encounter as a sweet little six-year-old. Although Yvonne had found it difficult to believe her daughter to begin with, she soon realised that her first thoughts of imaginary friends had been wrong and from that point wanted to help Melody to understand what was happening.

Yvonne had found Stella from an advert in the local Gazette. When she had called Stella and explained, Stella had been on the doorstep fifteen minutes later. She had been as old then, as Melody was now and both Melody and her mum had hit it off with Stella straight away.

Stella wore a long, flowing, flowery skirt with a tassel belt and flowery pumps. Her white, cheesecloth top had small daisies embroidered around the sleeves and a silver wing hung around her neck on a long, silver chain. She had also smelt different to anyone Melody had ever met before, a sweet but slightly musty smell and over her shoulder hung a small bag on a really long strap. Flowers encircled her long, flowing, blonde hair which framed her beautiful face.

Stella had looked at Melody, deep into Melody. Melody felt as though Stella was searching through her very soul and Melody had no defence against it. Stella had only looked at Melody for seconds, that to Melody had felt like an eternity.

"You are a rare one Melody, that's for sure!"

"Can you help her?"

The desperation had oozed out of my mother on that first afternoon.

"I can work with Melody, perhaps give her some tips on how to keep control, techniques to help Melody keep them out if she doesn't want to be disturbed but with this rare gift Melody might find it harder than most to keep them out. She's a healer. Not a healer of the living sick but a healer of the departed.

Yvonne hadn't been sure that she had understood Stella but as Stella had been prepared to help Melody then Yvonne couldn't ask for more.

The first time Melody had visited Stella's house Melody had been in total awe. The little cottage had a small, squeaky wooden gate that opened up onto an old brick path. Either side of the path wildflowers covered the flower patches. There was no lawn at all and some of the flowers had towered above Melody. Her mother was holding her hand tightly, her fear visible in that grip but Melody just felt a peaceful calm.

She saw a young girl, maybe just a little older than Melody, stood in the corner of the garden but the little girl wasn't wearing clothes that looked like any Melody had seen or worn. Her dress was almost to the floor and a white pinafore covered most of the dress. Beneath the skirt of her dress was a pair of boots. Melody could see laces and funny little hooks to hold the boots together. Her hair was long, blonde, and looked rather straggly and dirty. Melody had smiled at the girl, but the girl had just looked back, looked through her.

"Oh, what a shame," said Melody to her mother.

"What's a shame Melody?"

"That little girl can't find her mummy!"

"What little girl?"

"That one Mummy," as Melody pointed to where the little girl stood. Yvonne had physically blanched and the grip on Melody's hand had tightened.

At that moment the front door had opened, and Stella had noticed the direction that Melody and

Yvonne had been looking before they had both turned towards her.

“I see you’ve met Winifred,” and Stella had smiled towards the little girl. She won’t hurt you. She’s just looking for her mother so comes to check out anyone who comes through the gate, just in case.”

Yvonne looked both shocked, terrified, and confused all at the same time.

“Don’t worry Yvonne. With Melody’s gift you will soon get used to them being around even if you can’t see them.”

Yvonne thought that this was something she would never get used to and thanked the Lord that she could not see them.

Melody had followed Stella into that little cottage and looked around her. It was beautiful. There were crystals hanging in the windows and the light refracting through them made little coloured lights dance around the room. There had been a fireplace along one wall and along the top of the mantlepiece had been more crystals and candles too. Thick candles with ribbons of wax running down them, well used and some with not much life left in them.

The settee was all bright colours and a lovely bright rag rug lay on the stone floor in front of the fire.

The room had that same, sweet, musty smell that Melody had first smelt on Stella and in the corner of the room, a small bowl of dry leaves gently smouldered and tendrils of smoke twirled upwards into the room before dissipating, leaving just a faint haze across the room.

Stella had talked to Melody for a long time and the little girl was overjoyed with her new friend and couldn't wait for the next time they would be able to visit.

~

Stella answered the phone of the third ring.

“Hello Darling! What a wonderful surprise. How are you and how is that hunk, Ethan?”

“Hello Stella. I’d love to say ok but there is no point talking to you is there, you know me too well, but at least Ethan is still a hunk!” Melody laughed and Ethan could hear Stella laughing on the other end of the phone.

“Don’t mind me girls! I’m only here, hearing everything you’re saying,” but he was laughing too. He’d met Stella several times since meeting Melody and he had loved her as much as Melody, right from the first meeting. Stella had also made it very clear that Ethan was perfect for Melody.

“So, what’s up then girl?”

“I’ve been having a new visitor but it’s not like any of the others and Ethan has experienced this one with me too! I don’t see the spirit, neither did Ethan but we both smelt it and oh my God, it made me physically sick last night and we were both gagging over it a few minutes ago.”

Stella listened intently with just an occasional mmm or ooh.

“The scariest thing Stella, was that where I’d been sick last night, this thing walked through it, and I could see huge footsteps. This thing must have been a giant. Ethan took some pictures of it.”

“Wow, I’ve seen and heard a lot of things Melody but this one is even new to me, but I might be able to help, at least I know someone who might be able to help. Send me the pictures and I will have a word with Oscar. He might be more clued up on this.”

“Thanks Stella, I’ll send them straight over and wait to hear from you.”

"Of course, Lovely and you take care of that hunk of yours."

With that the call ended and Melody sat looking at Ethan as he continued along the road.

The day would have been a lovely treat had it not been marred with the events of the night before and the journey there. Melody felt an uneasy sense of foreboding with this visitation. She could not wait for Stella to get back to her with some information from Oscar. That worried her more than anything. She had heard Stella talking about Oscar and knew that he was what was known as a demonologist. Melody did not want to find that she had gained that sort of attachment.

That night Ethan stayed over and thankfully there were no bad smells through the night although the old man had returned but again said nothing. Ethan had slept through that visit. He must have felt the chill in the air though, as he had pulled the duvet tighter into his neck even though he was still fast asleep. Melody snuggled up to him and soon fell back to sleep.

“I’ve got to go Mel; I’ll see you later though.”

He kissed her gently then headed for the door.

Her phone started ringing and an unknown number flashed upon the screen. Although unknown, it was a local area code and Melody guessed it was Oscar and her heart plunged despite wanting to know what was going on.

“Hello Melody, Oscar here. Stella sent me the pictures and briefly told me what’s happened.

I can’t be sure, but I think I might have some good news for you.”

“Oh, I hope so Oscar. I don’t usually fear the other side, but this was something else and not very pleasant.”

“No, I can’t imagine it was very pleasant but the fact that nothing else happened makes me believe that it is still a spirit in need of healing. Usually, people who have had encounters such as yours, get scratched or something in the room gets moved or thrown. As none of that happened, I think you might just have to find a way of getting past the stench until it has delivered the message you need to help give it peace.”

“Thanks Oscar, that is good news, sort of! But I am really grateful for your time.”

“No problem, Melody. If the situation changes then I’ll do all I can to help you, but I hope you won’t need me at all now.”

Ethan came home later that evening and handed Melody a small, brown, crumpled, paper bag. It had clearly been in Ethan’s pocket and Emily peeped inside, only to find a small tub of Vicks VapoRub. Melody looked at him quizzically.

"I've been told that it helps to keep the smell out, thought it might be worth a try."

"That's so thoughtful of you."

She smiled the broadest smile that he loved. It lit up the whole room when she smiled like that, and Ethan couldn't help pulling her into his arms and giving her the biggest kiss.

"Well, if I'm going to be around next time that thing turns up, I want some protection too."

He'd laughed mischievously and Melody scoffed.

"Great, it wasn't a present for me at all then!"

The rain was hammering against the windowpanes, its rhythm fast and punchy. The air had cooled, and the wind had started howling like a banshee around the corner of the top storey apartment. Melody shuddered.

What had started out as a beautiful sunny day had resulted in an ear-splitting thunderstorm. The lightning had lit up the flat, creating shadows where there were none and in those instant flashes Melody was sure she had seen some one stood at the back of the kitchen, someone very large, and very dark. But because the flashes were so quick Melody couldn't be sure of what she had seen or if she had seen anything at all. Maybe it had just been her mind playing tricks on her. The lightning had been followed by the largest rumbles of thunder, the storm right above the flat, as the walls shook under the pressure created by the thunderclap. Melody did not like it at all. She never had liked that kind of storm, but recent events had made her more than a little nervous.

Then out of the kitchen walked the old man.

~

The pub was heaving. Every table was rammed and not an inch of the old wooden floorboards could be seen. Beer was being spilt by a rowdy group of youths and the music from the live band, set up in the farthest corner of the bar, was being drowned out by the chattering and laughter.

A small group of girls were celebrating a hen do. The bride-to-be wearing skirt far too short to be called a skirt with a boob tube, a large white sash with the words Bride-to-be and a tiara and veil. The girls all cheered as the cork was popped and the champagne flutes were lifted.

The bar was three people deep already and it was only seven thirty in the evening. The bar manager sighed, at least the takings would be good tonight, he thought.

Dave sat at a small, round table. The tabletop was covered in bright coloured tiles and atop of the tiles were at least fifteen empty glasses and Dave's pint.

He had chosen the busiest night of the week, a bar packed to the rafters, but Dave felt like the loneliest man on the planet. It was not the lack of a girlfriend that made Dave feel so lonely. In fact, his long-term girlfriend of thirteen years had almost insisted on joining Dave, but Dave had managed to dissuade her at the last minute. Marie was quietly relieved but concerned all the same.

The girl from behind the bar, with the bright green hair and super crazy make-up, strolled over to his table to collect the empty glasses. Dave kept his head down. He wouldn't have heard her if she had spoken to him anyway. His hearing had never been the same since joining the Royal Artillery. He had been a gunner for 9 years and had loved every moment of it. Could not imagine life on civvy street. Marie had been very patient with him, hoping that one day he would leave, and they would be able to settle in one town and maybe get married, even have kids. But he was only twenty-seven and not ready for that just yet.

No, his loneliness was not of a romantic nature at all. It was however, for a love lost. And that love had belonged to his Grandad.

Wilfred had been Dave's rock, his go to, his best friend, his confidante, his substitute father by all accounts. Dave's dad had left him and his mum when Dave was just starting school. He had little recollection of him, never tried to see him and had been more than happy when Grandad Wilfred had stepped up to the mark. Grandad Wilfred had been such a kind soul. He had loved Dave as though he was his own son. He had taught him all the things a father should teach his son and was so proud of Dave as he sat watching as his grandson at his passing out parade. The grandson who he thought of as his boy. To make Wilfred even more proud was that Dave had been awarded with 'best gunner' in his platoon.

They had partied hard that night. A big tear rolled down Dave's cheek and he brushed it quickly away with the back of his hand.

He had been overseas when Wilfred had suffered a huge heart attack at the age of seventy-two. He had died instantly, without warning and without the chance to say goodbye to his beloved boy,

Although the powers that be had tried to get Dave back in time, it didn't happen and by the time Dave got back to the UK, his grandad was in the earth and the flowers that covered his grave had all wilted and were turning brown. His mum had held her lad tight as the tears had flowed as he stood looking at those miserable, brown flowers.

And so it was that Dave sat alone, thinking about his beloved Grandad Wilfred when Melody walked in.

~

The bar was heaving. Ethan and Melody had heard the beat of the music from half a mile away but had not anticipated the number of punters there would be for a Thursday evening.

As Melody walked in through the small stable like front door, Ethan close on her heels, she stopped dead. Ethan nearly knocked her over. He had been turning back, closing the door, and had not seen her stop.

"Whoa Mel! Nearly knocked you over. What's the matter?"

Melody did not hear Ethan. Melody was staring at a table where a guy was sitting alone. Just a table full of empty glasses in front of him. His eyes, Ethan noticed were red and his hand kept wiping across them.

"Do you know him?" Ethan asked.

Melody still did not hear him. Behind the table where the guy was sitting stood the old man. The old man's hand seemed to be resting on the shoulder of the young man, the faint glow lighting up the side of his face, but the young man seemed to have no idea that he was there and neither did Ethan.

"Mel, earth to Mel, come in Mel"

"The old man is here."

"What old man?" Ethan looked puzzled.

"The old man that's been visiting me at night!"

Melody inched her way into the packed bar and headed toward the table where the young man was sitting. He looked up as Melody stood directly in front of him.

“Hi,” she said in her most compassionate voice.

“My name is Melody. Would you mind if Ethan, my partner, and I joined you?”

“Hmmm?”

“Join you? Do you mind if we join you?” Melody had raised her voice to be heard over the loud, raucous bar,

“No, feel free, name’s Dave but I’ll be going as soon as the bottom of this glass is empty. Table will be all yours then.”

“Actually,” said Melody, “We don’t want your table, it was you that I wanted, well, wanted to speak to, anyway.”

Melody smiled awkwardly. That had not come out at all right, but she continued as Ethen pushed his way through to the bar and bought them all a drink.

“I know I’m going to sound like a complete loony, but have you lost someone recently?”

Dave looked at her then, really looked at her. He didn’t know what to say. He didn’t want to say yes and open himself up to some charlatan, but he couldn’t help but notice the really tender look in Melody’s eyes. He said nothing.

“It’s just that,” continued Melody, used to the silence that often followed her initial question,

“It’s just that, well, you see, well no you can’t see but there is a gentleman stood right behind your shoulder.”

Dave turned to look at his left shoulder, then slowly turned towards his right.

“Sorry love, I don’t see anyone.” Dave’s head dropped back down towards the table and the old man started to show Melody everything that she needed.

“You’re a gunner, aren’t you? Been in the Forces some time! Your Grandad was so proud of you.”

Melody smiled at the image the old man had given her of the parade that had made Dave’s grandad so proud. Dave looked up and stared at Melody. He silently nodded.

“I don’t think you got back in time, did you? I don’t think your grandad had a chance to say goodbye.”

The tears that occasionally spilled over Dave’s eyes were now streaming down his face, A few people around the room had glanced over at Dave but Ethan walked over and blocked their view. He handed Dave the refill.

“You’re going to need this!” said Ethan as he passed over the pint.

“Your grandad, do you mind me asking his name?”

“Wilfred, Grandad Wilfred,” Dave whispered just loud enough for Melody to hear.

“Well Grandad Wilfred has been visiting me for a while now. He wants me to tell you that it’s ok that you didn’t get back in time. He is always right beside you and he wants you to know how extremely proud of you he has always been, from the moment your dad left you, right up until this very day. Your Grandad loves you so much and doesn’t like to see you so sad. He said just speak to him, he’s always listening even if you can’t see him!”

Dave leaned over and put his arms around Melody.

"I don't know how you know all that," Dave said as he choked back more tears, "But nobody knew about my dad. Thank you!"

Grandad Wilfred walked around the table and kissed Melody on the cheek. She didn't feel it, but she could see the glow as he came towards her, and she smiled at the old man.

"He's here?" asked Dave.

"Yes," said Melody.

But as she said that Wilfred turned and walked into the throng of people in the bar and was gone.

"He's left you know, but he's never far away, none of them are.

They carried on drinking and chatting throughout the rest of the evening. When it was finally time to go, they parted company and Dave left them with the first smile that had danced across his face in weeks.

~

Late Summer began to flow seamlessly into Autumn and as the cooler sunshine dipped down Melody shuddered at the blanket of cold air that wrapped itself around her shoulders. She hated leaving Summer behind and the first leaves falling from the trees were the tears that the season shed.

Melody had decided to walk home today. The streets were packed, pedestrians everywhere and the roads were nose to tail with commuters, blasting their horns and revving their engines noisily, in an attempt to push the traffic along, to get them back home to their warm houses sooner. It wasn't helping. Whatever was holding up the traffic must have been big.

Melody had seen the queues from her office window and knew the bus would be stuck for hours if it turned up at all. She had clearly made the right choice as not a single car or lorry had moved the entire time she had been walking. Because people couldn't see what the holdup was, they did not turn their engines off and the exhaust fumes were beginning to tickle the back of her throat.

Melody got a strange prickling feeling in the back of her neck. The feeling that eyes were boring into the back of her head, willing her to turn around. When she did turn around, the pavement behind her was rammed, pedestrians like sardines, all crammed onto the three-foot-wide pavement. Most heads were looking towards their feet, letting the crowd carry them along, like a surge of tidal water. However. one head stood out from the others. It was a good five inches taller than the average pedestrian and while that tidal wave of people continued to flow, that head was perfectly still. His head was bald. His eyes were just black sunken holes, just gnarly sockets where eyes should have been yet still Melody felt that this thing was staring at her and the shivers that ran through her body had nothing to do with the cool Autumn air.

Melody picked up the pace although her gut feeling was that it didn't matter how fast she moved, he would still be there, just a few feet away. The crowd was starting to thin. Melody could now see gaps on the pavement, not just the feet of the person in front of her. She had passed the butcher's shop with its bright, striped sun visor and plastic sheep stood guard in the entrance way. Melody then passed Bright Cuts, her hairdressers, the girls all busy with different customers, none of them saw her as she turned toward the window then looked back again over her shoulder.

Those gnarly, staring eyes were no longer visible above the crowd. Melody thought that maybe she had imagined it. A flashing red light caught her eye from the road ahead and as Melody neared, she heard loud voices above the crowd.

“Keep those people back! Make room for the ambulance. Hey Steve, over here mate?”

The flashing lights were getting brighter, and an acrid smell hung through the air. Melody found that her eyes were starting to smart, and she rubbed at them with the back of her hand. The Bank House was the last building in the row of shops and Melody passed it, getting closer to the flashing lights. As she started to turn the corner at the end of the road, the sight that met her eyes stopped her dead. Three cars were strewn across the road, one on its roof, the other two pummelled out of shape, smashed glass laying all around, belongings from the vehicles tossed around and strewn across the road and pavement.

There seemed to be people everywhere, running with equipment or stopping pedestrians going any further. A small boy sat crying on the side of the road, a policeman and his mother either side of him. When Melody looked closer the policeman was Ethan and the mother was stood just a little too close to the child. As she turned her arm, with a beautiful Rolex watch at the wrist, went straight through her son who didn't even notice. Nearby a stretcher was being loaded into the back of an ambulance, The sheet completely covering the victim but as the stretcher was jolted, the victim's hand dropped free of the cover and there was the watch that Melody had seen the mother wearing only seconds before.

People were being cut from the Toyota, that looked as though it had been spinning on its roof, and carefully laid upon the floor, immediately being completely covered by another ambulance crew while firefighters did what they needed to do to ensure that the vehicles didn't burst into flames.

Carnage!

And amid all that carnage was a very tall man who seemed to disappear and reappear with the flashing lights. As the flashing continued the gnarly eye sockets stared blankly at her through the chaos. A small group of people stood looking at the bodies lay out upon the floor. A group of people that shouldn't have been in the vicinity. A group of seeming bystanders that another ambulance crew member walked straight through, not even seeing them. Melody watched as the paramedic shuddered for no reason.

"Ethan, this is terrible! How on earth did this happen?"

"We aren't too sure at the moment. Are you ok?"

"I can see them all Ethan, the living, the dead, the emergency crews walking right through the departed! And when you were with that little chap, I could see his mother stood with you both."

Melody let out a sob.

"You need to go home Mel. I don't know what time I'll get off tonight, but I'll come straight round, if you want me to?"

"I don't want to go home. Right in the centre of all that carnage stood that stench from the other night. It was as though he was gloating. As though he had caused all that pain and suffering and wanted to somehow," Melody struggled to find the word, "well, just that. Gloat!"

"Oh Mel, that doesn't sound good!"

"I think I'm going to grab the car and head to Stella's. I'll call her on my way back and stay there tonight. I'm sure she won't mind."

"Ok love, drive carefully and I will see you tomorrow. If you feel you need to be there longer though, I understand"

"Thanks Ethan. You need to get back to helping those poor souls now, their need is greater than mine."

Ethan held her tight for just a second before turning away, back into the midst of the chaos. Melody looked towards the back of the ambulance where the tall man had stood. He was no longer there but she could still feel the gnarly, black eye sockets staring at her, or rather staring through her.

Stella was at the front door even before Melody had parked the car. She climbed out of her little Audi, pushed open the old, squeaky gate and headed up the old, brick path. More than twenty years after her first visit to Stella's cottage nothing had changed. Time seemed to have stood still in that little haven of the village.

"Come on love, kettle's on and you can stay as long as you need. Now, let's get that coat off you and get you in front of the fire. It's gone really nippy, rather quickly this year."

As they sat on that little colourful sofa, a little threadbare around the edges now but still just as comfy, they shared a pot of tea and Stella listened carefully.

"I just don't understand Stella. All of the spirits that usually visit me need a go between so that I can heal their wounds and give them peace in the afterlife. This is so much more, feels so wrong and I don't know how I can help!"

"I don't understand it either Melody. I don't believe I have come across anyone else who has had this kind of problem. While you're here though, we are going to do some deep meditation and some incantations to help raise your vibration level. Hopefully this will give you the power to protect yourself just in case this becomes violent."

"Thanks Stella. I really appreciate this and being able to stay with you. I know Ethan will be feeling better about it too. I knew, although he was desperate to get back to the incident, that he didn't want to leave me alone."

"I'm sure he didn't, and I wouldn't have liked the thought of you being alone either."

As Ethan's shift had changed to nights, Melody decided to stay with Stella for a whole week. She drove herself to work every day, then returned early evening to the calm, peace, quiet and protection of the cottage. Stella worked hard with Melody to raise her vibration levels and with the intense meditation, Melody was feeling stronger and more resilient every day. The week soon passed, and Melody hugged Stella hard before she headed out the door to return to her home.

Melody could see Stella waving, in her rear-view mirror as she drove off down the lane towards the bypass and home. As she pulled up outside the flat, she could see an ambient glow coming from the lounge. Her phone pinged just as she was switching the engine off.

‘Don’t Panic, Only Me’

Melody wasn’t expecting Ethan to be there until very late in the evening. Melody also didn’t expect to see the sight that met her eyes as she let herself into the flat. There were flower vases of every shape, size, and colour. Some were made of glass while others were different painted clay vases, and each filled with an array of flowers. It wasn’t just the sight of the beautiful colours and shades that blew her away but the smell that filled the rooms too. There were also candles everywhere, their dancing flames making the flowers look as though they too were dancing.

"Wow Ethan, these are all just gorgeous! But I don't know what I've done to deserve these, and they must have cost you a fortune!"

Ethan walked over to her and hugged her tight. "I have been so worried about you. I know you were safe with Stella, but I can't help but worry when I can't see what I need to protect you from. And I don't want anything to happen to you Mel. You are my whole world."

The weekend was delightful. Melody and Ethan did nothing at all. They ordered take away food and feasted on old movies. They had lay-ins that lasted until lunchtime and cosied on the sofa in their pyjamas. Melody saw no spirits and the tall man didn't show at all. There were no terrible stenches and Melody secretly hoped that she had seen the last of that spirit.

The following week was also eventless, and Melody was really beginning to relax until she came home from work as the end of the week was drawing near. The ambient glow was once again coming from the windows of her lounge. Melody knew however, that Ethan was working late that evening and wouldn't be home until after ten. She headed up the staircase to her front door. As she pushed the key in the lock, she noticed that the faint glow, showing through the crack under the door, had suddenly shut off. Melody's heart plummeted. She pushed the front door open, and the stench hit her again. It got up inside her nostrils and caught in the back of her throat. The sight that met her eyes caused her to take a sharp intake of breath and a small scream escaped her.

Every single one of the beautiful flowers, the flowers that had still been perfect blooms when she had left them that morning, had withered to the point that they had gone crisp. That would normally take weeks to reach that point. On seeing the flowers, the realisation dawned on Melody was that the stench was the water that the flowers had been standing in. In the glass vases, Melody could see that the water had turned black even though it had been crystal clear that morning. Some of the flowers had lost their petals completely and the room was a disaster zone.

Melody instinctively knew what or who had caused her beautiful blooms to all wither and die. She went into the kitchen, grabbed a binbag from the draw and began to empty the vases. As she picked up bunch after bunch, the putrid water had congealed. It didn't drip from the bottom of the flowers, but fell and splodged like slime, sticking to her carpets, and leaving horrible black stains upon her furniture. Her eyes were watering from the smell, so she didn't notice the tears as they slid down her cheeks. It was as she got to the last vase that the pungent aroma of the dripping slime morphed into the stench of a thousand dead corpses. Her skin prickled, the hairs on the back of her neck and her arms stood tall and the air around her went frigid once more.

She did not have to turn around to know that the tall man was behind her. Every ounce of her being was screaming at her. She was terrified. She knew she needed to turn around and face this. Her mind was willing her to run. Her body was ignoring all commands and had frozen on the spot. The air around her was getting colder and colder. Tendrils of her breath were rising into the air. Then she felt an ice-cold hand on her shoulder. She screamed so loud that seconds later there was a loud banging on her door. Her neighbour burst into the room. The freezing hand on her shoulder evaporated and Melody's knees gave way as she sunk to the floor, surrounded by slime and black bin bags.

There had to be an answer, a clue as to what this spirit wanted, but Melody could not think what it might be. The flowers were no clue. Just the freezing cold chill in the air would have caused the flowers to wither and the spirit's presence and stench was enough to turn anyone into a putrid, slimy mess. It had to be something else.

That night as Melody slept, her mind saw a mass of jumbled images. None of it made any sense to her. There were people that she hadn't recognised, places that she couldn't recall having been to and events happening that had never happened to her. There was, however, a family. The family consisted of two beautiful daughters with stunning, long, blonde hair. Each girl a small, identical image of their mother. And then there was the tall man. This tall man was not a grotesque monster. This tall man was attractive. This tall man had a handsome face with beautiful hazel eyes and dark hair. This tall man smelt of freshly applied aftershave. His skin was smooth and clear, and it was very clear to Melody that this tall man loved his family dearly as he had swooped up his daughters, one at a time and spun his wife around as they had walked in a park. A park, Melody noticed, that was full of beautiful flowers of every colour and every shade. And even though Melody was still dreaming she could smell every single bloom as though someone was holding each flower under her nose.

All the love of that man and that family hung heavily in the air as Melody opened her eyes. The light was pouring into the room, from the brilliant sunshine outside and Melody, for the first time, felt that she had seen into the life of the tall man and knew what she had to do next.

The day was beautiful. The sun shone brightly in the sky. The rain and the cold weather had seemed to vanish, taking Autumn back with it and Summer had returned with a smile on its face and sand between its toes. Even the leaves that had turned seemed to shine from the trees, there beautiful, golden display even brighter, the rich shades of red, even richer and the air clear and crisp.

Melody breathed in this beautiful day as she walked along the unusually quiet main road. The bakers shop heralded its arrival with the sweet smell of freshly baked bread and Trish waved through the window at her.

Melody continued on her journey. The library was silent as Melody walked in. You would have heard more than a pin drop. There was only one other person in the large, shelf filled room that morning and that was the middle-aged lady behind the desk. Melody had not been into the library for possibly three years and did not know the librarian at all. Her small, piercing eyes looked out at Melody, through her turtle-shell spectacles with the silver chain hanging loosely around her neck. Her blouse had a high, ruffled collar. Her green cardigan matched the green skirt which Melody guessed, matched the green shoes, although she couldn't see her feet.

"Good morning. I'd like to do some research if that's possible?"

Only then did the librarian smile and instantly her whole face warmed and that stern façade seemed to melt away. She showed Melody how to use the new Digital Microfilm Viewer-Scanner System. Melody discovered that she was the first to use the new equipment before the librarian left her to begin her search.

It was a mammoth job. Melody scanned through article after article but was hindered by the fact that she didn't really know what she was looking for. The seconds turned into minutes, minutes into hours and soon the day had passed with no answers and Melody left the library a little down hearted, but she knew how to proceed and who to turn to next.

It was Monday before Melody could move forward and the phone was answered instantly.

“William Nichols, Standard and Gazette, how can I help you?”

“Hello Billy.”

There was a silent pause at the other end of the line. Melody’s heart began to hammer just a little too hard. She knew it had been a long time but hadn’t thought that Billy wouldn’t want to speak to her. Maybe she had misjudged things terribly. Just as these thoughts were hurtling around Melody’s head a large burst of laughter erupted from the receiver.

“Smelly Mellie! Darling girl, how the devil are you? I can’t believe it. What is it now, seven years, eight years?”

“Ah come on Billy. Don’t go flattering yourself. You and I are the same age, left college at the same time and you know as well as I do that it’s eleven years since those good old days with Mr Perkins!”

“Ha Yeh, good old gherkins Perkins. Where would we be without him eh? So Smelly, what can I do for you my lovely girl or were you just missing Billy’s southern drool?”

“How are you at research these days Billy? You always were the best.”

“Well, I had enough practice doing all your research, Andy’s research and trying to fit in my own. You two should have been barred and I should have got three passes on that course.”

“Come on Billy, you loved it. Anything to spend time ogling that bloke in the library, what was his name?”

“Oh, you dreadful girl. How could you bring Antonio back up and break my heart all over again?”

It was Melody’s turn to laugh and after a few minutes of catching up she explained what she needed Billy to do for her. She knew he had left college and gone to work for the paper and had done really well. He had such a way that people would tell him anything and his reporting skills were renowned in the area.

“Anything for you Smelly but it’s going to cost you darling!”

“Name it, Billy.”

“We must go out and have a good old knees up. I’ll bring Jezza and you can bring what’s his name. What is his name?”

“Ethan! His name is Ethan and of course we will go out on the razzle dazzle with you. In fact, I can’t wait. What about this weekend? Hopefully you will have found out what I need to know too by then."

"Ok darling. It's a date and I'll see what I can dig up for you."

The line went dead, and Melody smiled thinking about her old friend. If anyone could find out about the tall man it would be Billy, she thought.

The week dragged by, even though Melody tried to keep herself busy. She was so desperate to get some answers and to find a way of helping the restless spirit of the tall man to find peace. She had walked through the door on Wednesday and that putrid smell had met her on the threshold and had assaulted her nostrils straight away. This time however, the putrid, rank smell was much milder than it had been before, and Melody only had to open the windows for a few minutes for the stench to clear. She felt that that, in itself, had been a good sign. Maybe the tall man knew too that his torture was somehow drawing to a close, that Melody had, in fact found a way to help him even though she didn't know it herself at that moment.

The weekend finally arrived, and Ethan got ready to take Melody to the little French restaurant on the High Street. The Blue Moon was busy as always, but Melody had booked the best table in the restaurant, situated near the back but in a small annex that only housed the one, large, wooden table and a beautiful, double, sliding, patio door which opened out on to a cobblestoned, patio area that could have stepped straight out of Paris itself. The table was laid for four, with three different glasses at each setting, which sparkled under the brilliant light of the chandelier hanging just above the table, almost touching the small Eiffel Tower at the centre piece. The knives and forks were silver-plated with beautiful, ornate designs on them, and the napkins were deep blue edged in red and white ribbon.

Ethan had already ordered a bottle of wine for the table and the Jean Foillard Morgon Cote du Py was waiting for them on the table. Billy walked up to the table and whistled.

"Ohh la laa! Tres bien, mon prefere."

"Oh Billy, you are such a smooth talker but I'm glad you like Ethan's choice of wine. He spent a couple of years in France, touring the vineyards and notorious wine regions and came away with some really tasty choices."

They ordered their food and as the meals began to arrive Melody started to feel super impatient.

"Come on then Billy, what did you find out for me? What started out as a terrifying ordeal has ended up being the one soul, I want to help the most, especially after the dream about his beautiful family."

"You'd best brace yourself for this Smelly. This is the most heart-breaking story I have ever come across in all my years of journalism.

It started twenty years ago..."

~

Martin met Isla at college. They fell in love instantly and all their family and friends knew that they were going to spend the rest of their lives together. They were married the week after they had both graduated from university and they settled into a beautiful town house in Bath.

Martin was a defence lawyer and Isla was a dental nurse. They both loved their jobs, but Isla couldn't wait to start a family. Eighteen months later Annabelle was born, a healthy little girl and the love of their life. Two years later, Isla gave birth to

Claudia. In her mind their family was now complete, and Martin doted on all of his girls. He was so full of love for these three, beautiful women, as little as two of them were, that he didn't think life would get any better than that. Sadly, it didn't.

Martin had continued his job. He had started defending this evil man known by the name of Hunch. Hunch was a serial rapist and Martin knew by looking at the scum bag that he was guilty. The evidence however, said differently and Martin should have defended this man easily. His moral compass had led him down a different path and he refused to act for this vile excuse for a human being.

They had found Martin in his chambers late in the evening of the day that he had stepped down from the case. He had been badly beaten, lay unconscious and his personal belongings had been taken. Amongst those things had been his house keys. Nobody knew who had done this to him and nobody knew how long Martin had been unconscious or when the attack had taken place. What people hadn't observed that afternoon was that a member of the public, a friend of Hunch, had crept out of the hearing after Martin had resigned and waited in a very dark corner of the court house until everyone except Martin had left.

Meanwhile, Hunch had escaped from the court and had gone into hiding very close to the building he had escaped from. A bold move that had paid off. He had been passed the house keys and had gone around to Martin's house as soon as the cover of darkness had allowed him too.

When the alarm had eventually been raised about Martin, it had been too late. Hunch had let himself into the house and killed his wife and children.

The autopsy report concluded that his wife had been repeatedly raped and strangled. His daughters had also been strangled and had been found tied to chairs facing the direction of where their mother had had the life squeezed out of her. What had sickened and tortured Martin the most was that the autopsy report also stipulated that his wife's demise had come before that of his children. That sick, evil monster had made those girls watch.

Martin had been beside himself. He had demolished several bottles of whiskey a week in those first few weeks. He was a wreck without his beautiful family, and it had eaten him alive that, not only had he not been able to stop it from happening but if he hadn't resigned from the case, Hunch would never have touched any of them. It was all his fault, and he knew that he would never be able to live with that desperate feeling of loss and betrayal.

And so it was, in a whiskey fuelled stupor, that Martin had taken himself off to the woodland on the edge of town, climbed a big old oak tree with a long length of thick rope over his shoulder, tied one end of the rope to the branch and the other around his neck, and slid silently off the branch.

His weight had caused his neck to snap instantly. His eyes had bulged slightly. The tree he had chosen was in a dense part of the woodland, a part never visited by walkers or passers-by. It wasn't even visible from the nearest well-worn footpath. And so it was that Martin hung there for several weeks before he had been found. It had been a hot summer too and as the hot sunshine bore down onto his body, decay had started to happen rapidly. The birds had also pecked his eyeballs out of their sockets and his hair had all dropped out of his head.

The putrid stench of decay had been overbearing when he had eventually been found. His body was unrecognisable to the living and breathing Martin of just a few weeks before. He had eventually been buried in a completely different graveyard to his wife and children.

~

The tears streamed down Melody's cheeks as Billy finished telling this horrific tale. Melody could not get to grips with the fact that this had been a true story that she had never heard of before. Billy reminded her that it had happened before Melody had even been born so it was hardly surprising that she hadn't heard about it. It hadn't happened in their little town either.

Billy handed Melody a piece of paper as they eventually left the restaurant. Melody apologised for not wanting to go clubbing and they went their separate ways. The following day Melody jumped in her car.

"Are you sure you don't want me to come with you? It's quite a drive!"

"Don't worry Ethan. I'll be fine. I'll let you know when I'm on my way back or if I think I might have to stop over."

With that Melody had sped off into the distance.

The roads had been heaving all the way and Melody was exhausted by the time she had got to the little village church. She sat collecting her thoughts for a few moments when the pungent smell of death, once more enveloped her but this time she was ready for it and turned to the tall man who sat just inches away from her in the passenger's seat, his gnarled eye sockets seeming to plead with her.

"You are going to have to trust me and follow me and we are both going to have to hope for the best."

The tall man hung his head. As Melody climbed out of the car, he was suddenly right behind her. The sun was beginning to fade, and the shadows of the yew trees dappled over the gravestones. Melody knew her search would have to be quick, worried that the light would fade too quickly, and she hadn't thought to pick up a torch. Her worries were futile.

As Melody rounded the corner of the grey, stone church, there, in the furthest corner of the graveyard, were three figures. Two were sitting next to a beautiful, white, marble angel, while the third, a beautiful little girl, with long blonde hair, jumped through the angel.

Melody heard a gasp behind her. She looked back expecting to see the monster

but there, stood Martin, staring at his wife and daughters.

Claudia spotted him first.

“Daddy!” she cried and started to run towards them. Melody could see Isla clearly now. There was a beautiful smile upon her face and not a trace of accusation towards her husband for not being there for them. She just radiated pure love.

She watched as the family reunited, just before a ray of sunshine glinted in Melody’s eyes and then they were gone. As Melody climbed back into the car the local Gazette caught her eye. The front cover had a report covering the inquest into the accident that had happened on her local High Street. It was a name that had caught her eye.

‘A prison escapee, who had evaded recapture for more than thirty years and who went by the name of Hunch was the pedestrian who had been caught up in the middle of a three-car accident on High Street, an inquest heard yesterday. He died instantly along with three of the passengers of the vehicle. The cause of the accident has not been established.’

Melody smiled.

www.ingramcontent.com/pod-product-compliance
Lightning Source LLC
LaVergne TN
LVHW052054160826
845678LV00015B/3217

* 9 7 9 8 8 3 5 6 0 2 4 8 3 *